MESOPOTAMIAN MANIA

WEAM NAMOU

HERMiZ
PUBLiSHING

Library of Congress Cataloging-in-Publication Data
2025900425

Namou, Weam

The Magical Museum
Mesopotamian Mania
(Middle Grade Fiction)

ISBN
978-1-945371-12-7 (paperback)
978-1-945371-13-4 (eBook)

First Edition

Published in the United States of America by:
Hermiz Publishing, Inc.
Sterling Heights, MI

10 9 8 7 6 5 4 3 2 1

For every child who hasn't yet learned that their story began thousands of years ago.

CONTENTS

MESOPOTAMIAN MANIA

PART 1

THE SUMERIANS

CHAPTER 1

The Welcoming Museum

I stood outside the majestic wooden doors. The mosaic lion, made of golden glazed bricks, stared at me. I stared back, admiringly. Around the lion, the name of the Chaldean Museum glistened in a royal font. It featured both English and Aramaic letters, the language of Jesus. I adjusted my blazer and smoothed my long, straight hair. The gold necklace and bracelets from Baghdad jingled as I checked my phone for the time. Ten sixth graders were due any minute.

Soon, I heard the chatter of young students approaching. I circled the museum, entering through the back. From a distance, Mr. Yatooma's boisterous voice carried across the courtyard as he organized his students for a photo. His tall, slender figure and dark features, including a prominent mustache, stood out as he gestured enthusiastically. Nearby, Helen, the parent chaperone, was a red-haired woman with glasses. She quietly organized the students, casting sidelong glances at Mr. Yatooma as he animatedly directed the group.

I made my way through the museum. My heels clicked loudly against the marble floors, echoing through the silent galleries—echoes of the splendor of Babylon. I greeted the artifacts and objects as I passed. They greeted me in return. Arriving at the entrance, I opened the tall doors, and the children turned and looked at me.

"Welcome, children, to the world's first and only Chaldean Museum!" Stepping aside with a sweep of my arm, I welcomed them into the magnificent entryway filled with soft, melodic music.

The students filed in with the typical energy of a school day. Sunlight filtered through the tall glass panes, turning dust into miniature stars that seemed to follow the children's movements. Three caught my attention. Leading the group was Mary, athletic and confident, her dark hair cascading past her shoulders and her notebook clutched tightly. She wore dark jeans, a purple shirt, and bright red shoes that stood out. Following her was Zaya, medium-sized and grinning, his T-shirt half-untucked, and beside him was Lola. With her wavy light brown hair and bright, observant eyes, she moved quietly, taking everything in. She dressed in black tights and her own pair of vibrant red shoes that perfectly matched Mary's.

"Hello, everyone!" I said as the children gathered around. "My name is Weam, and I'm the Executive Director here at the Chaldean Museum. I'm also known as the Chaldean Storyteller."

The children stood transfixed, their gazes split between me and the flowing aqua drapes lining the wall. The sheer fabric danced gently in the air, shimmering like the Tigris and Euphrates Rivers.

"Before I begin," I said, "I'd like to know what you hope to gain from the experience of each of our six galleries. We'll start with this gallery, Ancient Mesopotamia, and share our other goals as we move along."

Mary opened her notebook. "I need to find an interesting history project," she said, her pencil hovering over the pristine page.

"I'm dying to know if the ancient Chaldeans vanished—" Zaya began, making a puff gesture with his hands. The ceiling lights flickered briefly, matching his dramatic timing.

"Or if aliens helped them build their empire," Lola cut in softly, her eyes drawn to the strange patterns the artifacts' shadows cast on the floor.

Their statements sparked a wave of excitement, voices bouncing off the stone walls.

Mr. Yatooma made several quick, sharp claps. "Everyone, quiet!" he commanded, like a military sergeant.

Helen's hand went to her chest, startled. The space fell still.

"Is this going to take a long time?" Zaya interrupted.

Mr. Yatooma stepped forward, his eagerness evident. "It'll take as long as it takes, and you won't want to miss a moment!"

Helen adjusted her glasses with a slight eye roll.

Oh, Lord, I thought as I studied the group before me—Mary's intense focus, Zaya's half-grin, half-curious expression, and Lola's piercing gaze that seemed to see right through me. These weren't the usual casual questions I encountered. These children were hungry for real answers. I instinctively touched my pendant for reassurance.

"Children, this tour will help answer some of your questions," I said. "But I want to stress that while this museum celebrates Chaldean heritage, its story belongs to all of humanity. You see, when someone in ancient Mesopotamia looked at a round object and thought, 'What if this could help us move things?'—they didn't just wonder. They carved wheels and transformed how humans could transport goods. When someone pressed a wedge-shaped stick into clay, they developed it into cuneiform, created schools, and built libraries. These weren't just Mesopotamian inventions; they were human breakthroughs that changed history."

"So we're like… guardians of history?" Lola asked, curiously.

Mary paused her writing to look up. Zaya leaned forward, his attention caught.

"The Mesopotamians left solid proof of creating many firsts," I said. "They documented their world, their ideas, their lives."

"That's why they were called the Cradle of Civilization," said Mr. Yatooma, pride resonating in his voice.

Helen adjusted her glasses and nodded, her earlier skepticism softening.

"Through these galleries," I gestured to the archway ahead, "we'll discover how ancient Mesopotamia grew through the work of inventors, writers, and dreamers. This isn't just about the past—it's about understanding how a group of people between two rivers shaped our world."

"It's why we're here today," Mr. Yatooma added, his voice firm. "To understand humanity's story, we must begin where it began."

CHAPTER 2

First Cities

I moved toward the large wall map of Mesopotamia. "We'll start in the Ancient Gallery with the Sumerians who lived in Sumer, in the southern parts of this region, where we trace our roots." My finger traced the area between the two rivers. "Before they became farmers, they were hunter-gatherers, roaming wherever food led them. But, as some scholars have noted, they weren't primitive nomads. Then, they discovered this land between the Tigris and Euphrates Rivers—the Fertile Crescent."

Mary jotted notes while Lola studied the map with keen eyes. Zaya lounged against a display case, but his attention remained fixed on the presentation.

"Guess what happened next?" I asked the group.

"Did they find magical treasures in the sand?" a student in the back asked.

"Not treasure," I said, "but something

better—agriculture! They no longer needed to search for food. Now, what happens when you have plenty to eat?"

"Bro, you get super lazy and lay on the couch," Zaya said, patting his stomach.

The class erupted in laughter.

"Yes, and you have time to be creative," I added. "They started building and inventing at remarkable speed. Picture a world over 5,000 years ago, with cities rising from the desert."

"So they built the first real cities?" Mary asked.

"Yes, Mary. Each city had its own god as protector. They had temples, walls, and an early form of democracy. Power was shared between religious leaders, citizens' councils, and kings."

"Were there women rulers?" Mary's question carried a note of hope.

"Women held power," I confirmed. "Actually, kings needed a goddess's blessing to rule."

Lola raised her hand. "Is that where the setup of kings and queens started?"

I shook my head. "Different rulers emerged worldwide. But the Mesopotamians left us the earliest written records of leadership."

The discussion continued until Zaya and several boys drifted toward Hammurabi's Stele, drawn to its digital display. Though they tried to suppress it, their laughter swept through the gallery like a sudden gust of wind.

"Boys," I called, pulling their attention back. Mr. Yatooma's stern voice and Helen's stern face helped restore order.

"Do those ancient cities still exist?" Lola asked.

"Yes and no," I answered. "The sites still exist as archaeological ruins in modern-day Iraq. But they're not living cities anymore."

"Can people visit them?" Mary asked.

"Unfortunately, many sites are closed to visitors due to regional conflicts," I explained. "But archaeologists continue their work when possible, uncovering new discoveries about our ancestors."

"Like Indiana Jones?" Zaya perked up.

"Real archaeologists work with more patience," Mr. Yatooma cut in with a laugh. "They spend months brushing dirt with small tools."

I walked to the trade routes map. "During their golden age, from 3300 to 2000 BC, cities like Ur, Uruk, and Eridu became centers of trade and culture. Ur holds special significance. It's known as Ur of the Chaldeans, Prophet Abraham's birthplace. This connects the Chaldeans to Judaism, Christianity, and Islam."

Mary's pen moved across the page in neat rows while Lola studied the trade routes with intense focus. Zaya had moved closer, his usual playfulness giving way to genuine interest.

"Now, let's travel in time to bustling urban hubs filled with towering temples called ziggurats," I said.

"Cigarettes?" Zaya said, nudging his friends.

"Zaya!" Helen's voice carried a warning as giggles rippled through the group.

"Zig-u-rat..." I pronounced.

"Eww, rat?" Zaya's friend covered his mouth.

"No, it's a zoo app!" another boy called.

"Boys, stop that!" Helen's patience wore thin.

"A Ziggurat," I explained, noticing that Mr. Yatooma was not intervening. Evidently, he found this humor amusing. "It was where priests and priestesses lived as mediators between people and gods."

"Like a magical tower reaching up to heaven?" Lola's eyes held their dreamy look.

"Yes," I said. "They believed the higher the building, the closer they were to God. Some historians think the Ziggurat might be the Tower of Babel."

Mary had to quicken her notebook skills to catch up with the information being shared. "So, it was their government and religious center?"

"Like the Vatican City today," I confirmed. "It stood as an independent territory with its own hospital and justice system."

A girl raised her hand. "Is that why they built them in steps? To climb closer to heaven?"

"Smart observation," I said, then scanned the room. "What structures does the Ziggurat resemble?"

"Stacks of *gubtah*?" someone called out in Chaldean, meaning cheese.

"Stacks of baklawa?" another added.

Laughter filled the gallery until Mr. Yatooma restored order.

"Pyramids?" several voices suggested.

"Not quite. Pyramids are triangular, but ziggurats are rectangular." I pointed to the display. "Have any of you seen Mayan temples?"

Recognition dawned in their faces.

"My cousin visited Chichen Itza last summer," someone said.

"You visited Chicken Pizza himself?" Zaya asked.

The class erupted in giggles.

"Chi-chen It-za," I enunciated carefully. "And these ziggurats actually came first. They're thousands of years older."

Oohs and aahs resonated across the gallery.

"What is this?" A student pointed to an encasement.

"The Marsh People," I said. "I call it the Venice of Iraq. They travel by canoe and build homes from straw, living as their ancestors did thousands of years ago."

"Are the Marsh Arabs descendants of the Sumerians?" asked Helen.

"Perhaps," I said and allowed for a long silence as everyone contemplated.

CHAPTER 3

Wheels and Words

"Now, what do you think is mankind's most important invention?" I asked.

Zaya bounced on his feet. "The remote control! Who wants to get up to change channels?"

The suggestions grew more creative.

"The snooze button!"

"Autocorrect!"

"Pizza delivery app!"

As laughter bounced through the museum, a girl with a rosary around her neck spoke softly in Chaldean, "*A'etah?*" meaning church.

"Well, children, those are excellent and creative answers," I said. "While they're amusing, there are older inventions that are pretty significant, like the wheel and writing."

"Ms. Weam, I read a great deal about the wheel," said Mary. "The inventors started rolling heavy objects with logs. Then someone had a brilliant idea—what if we made them thinner?"

"Like slicing pepperoni?" Zaya mimed cutting motions.

"Zaya, let her finish," said Helen, disapprovingly.

"I'm finished," said Mary with certainty.

Helen's brows furrowed further than usual.

"That's a wonderful explanation, Mary," I said. "Imagine where we'd be today without the wheel? Especially here in Michigan, with the auto industry."

"Yo, check this out!" Mr. Yatooma jumped in. "Before these sweet rides, people had to walk and walk and walk, for what seemed like eternity! Then the wheel changed everything—planes, strollers, wheelchairs. It's like the d—" He caught himself mid-word, as Helen's face transformed into the expression she usually reserved for cafeteria food fights.

Mr. Yatooma must be an enigma in his classroom—one moment wielding authority like a veteran principal, the next bouncing around with the energy of a caffeinated teenager. His teaching style might raise eyebrows at a school board meeting, but I'd take his authentic chaos over the robotic drone of my own childhood teachers any day.

Pushing those thoughts aside, I seized the moment to pivot our discussion.

"Let's talk about how humans first started writing things down," I said, reaching for my little museum bag. "Writing in ancient Mesopotamia started around 3200 BCE. The Sumerians created a system called cuneiform, which means 'wedge-shaped.'" I pulled out a replica stylus, holding it up like a conductor's baton. "They used a tool like this—called a stylus—to make marks in soft clay. Picture taking a marsh plant and cutting one end into a tiny triangle, like a prehistoric pen."

"*Kthawa d'teena*," Mr. Yatooma said, using the Chaldean words for clay writing.

"Teena?" Zaya, omitting the unpronounceable Arabic/Aramaic letters, pronounced the name so it sounded like the Chaldean word for urine. The children erupted in laughter.

Helen's sharp "Enough!" cut through the chaos, frightening even the teacher.

I stepped forward, commanding their attention before matters got out of hand. "Can anyone guess why they chose clay?"

"Because they didn't have paper?" Zaya offered, properly chastened.

"Paper hadn't been invented yet," I explained. "But clay was perfect—plentiful near the rivers, easy to shape, and when baked, it lasted forever. That's why we can still read their words today."

"But wouldn't the clay get mushy?" Mary asked, scribbling notes. She glanced at Zaya, adding, "By the way, *teena* has another definition—figs."

After the giggles subsided, I continued, "They used special clay and worked quickly, like Play-Doh before it dries. They could only fix mistakes while it was wet."

"Like when Mr. Yatooma makes us write in pen," Zaya groaned, triggering more laughs.

"At least you don't have to bake your homework!" Mr. Yatooma's hands flew up, shaping invisible clay. "As for the comparison with Play-Doh, of course, instead of bowls, the Sumerians were making grocery lists and epic adventures on the clay. If you messed up—" He clapped dramatically "—you just smooshed it and started over."

With that, I guided them to the clay tablets behind temperature-controlled glass.

"They're so tiny!" Lola leaned toward the display, her breath fogging the glass. "How did anyone read this?"

"With great difficulty," I said. "Scribes spent years learning cuneiform. It's estimated there are between half-a-million to two million cuneiform tablets that have been excavated."

"But only a fraction of them have been fully read and published," Mr. Yatooma interjected.

Helen cleared her throat to indicate improper behavior.

"What's this one about?" Mary asked, pointing to a well-preserved tablet.

"A receipt for sheep," I said. "You see, they wrote about everything from business deals to poetry, epics, and mathematical problems."

The tiny wedge-shaped marks shifted and settled in the dim light, as if listening and responding approvingly. I wondered if I was the only one who noticed.

"They invented writing just to make receipts?" Zaya snorted.

I shifted my attention away from the stirring words on the cuneiform tablet. "Actually, some of humanity's earliest writing was accounting. But they also wrote recipes for all sorts of meals and even for beer."

"Beer?" Several students perked up.

"Yes, and when people weren't happy with what they bought—whether it was beer, copper, or anything else—they did exactly what we do today. They complained. In fact, we have the world's first letter of complaint right here in clay."

"You do?" Mary asked, mesmerized.

"It all started with a merchant named Nanni. He needed copper and found a seller named Ea-nasir, so he sent his servant with money to make the purchase. But when his servant returned..." I paused for a moment. "The copper was wrong. All wrong. Not only that, but Ea-nasir had been rude to Nanni's servant!"

The children's faces showed their investment in the story.

"So Nanni did what any of us would do."

"What?" asked Lola.

"Well, he wrote a strongly worded letter. He pressed each mark into the clay, telling Ea-nasir exactly what he thought about the bad copper and the poor treatment of his servant. He demanded better copper and proper respect."

"Did he get his money back?" Zaya asked.

"We don't know. But Ea-nasir kept the complaint letter. Archaeologists found it in his house thousands of years later, along with other complaint letters from other unhappy customers. Seems Ea-nasir had quite a reputation for selling bad copper."

"He kept all the angry letters?" Lola asked, incredulous.

"An entire collection," I said, spreading my hands. "Four thousand years later, and people still write to companies about their complaints. So if you ever wonder where our love for complaining came from—it's in our bloodline!"

The adults snickered, and I could see the children's imaginations spinning with possibilities.

CHAPTER 4

Ancient Voices

"From this ancient land they discovered the oldest poem," I said.

"What kind of poem?" Helen asked, her scholarly interest piqued.

"A love poem." I grinned as several students made faces. "Picture this: A young woman is in love with King Shu-Sin. She takes a clay tablet and begins pressing words into it, each mark capturing her feelings. 'Bridegroom, dear to my heart,' she writes. 'Goodly is your beauty, honeysweet.'"

"Honeysweet?" Zaya wrinkled his nose.

"Oh yes. She goes on to call him her lion, dear to her heart. The entire poem is filled with honey and sweetness and all the ways she adores him."

Some of the kids looked mortified, while others seemed secretly fascinated. I paused, giving them a chance to recuperate.

"You know," I said, eyes twinkling, "this poem

could make a unique gift for your Valentine's Sweetheart, no?"

Laughter erupted, mixed with gasps and exaggerated grimaces. Some stuck out their tongues in disgust, others acted as if they would vomit.

"Imagine if we couldn't communicate through writing," I said. "Think about it—we'd have to talk all the time to share our ideas…"

"We could communicate through telepathy," Zaya suggested, surprising everyone with his thoughtful response.

"Ah, smart answer," I said. "And yes, that could work, but then we wouldn't have any books."

"And we'd lose all the stories," Lola added softly, her fingers tracing invisible words in the air. "All the dreams and memories people wrote…"

Mary jotted down 'alternative communication methods' in her notebook.

"Wait, where are the Chaldeans in all this?" he asked, peering into the dim corners of the room as if expecting answers to materialize.

Lola, her eyes filled with excitement, jumped in. "And did aliens contact them?" She grabbed Mary's notebook and flipped through her notebook where she'd been collecting questions since we started. "Didn't they also invent the sailboat? I keep picturing these ancient ships crossing rivers of stars…"

"Maybe…" Helen paused by a map of ancient trade routes. "That's why some ancient structures appear similar across different civilizations. The ideas sailed across oceans and rolled across deserts…"

"Or aliens helped them!" Lola rushed to join her at the map. "Think about it—all these amazing inventions, and they just happened to figure them out?"

Zaya peered over their shoulders. "I've seen stuff like that on the History Channel!"

"That's where I saw it!" Lola said, happily.

"Children," Helen started with a critical tone, but I held up my hand.

"No, this is good," I said. "Critical thinking is important. Lola, what makes you think aliens might have been involved?"

"Well, for the many reasons that can't be explained," she answered.

Mr. Yatooma stepped forward and pointed to different spots on the map. "Here are the reasons: How did they know about astronomy? How did they build such perfect structures? How did they understand mathematics so well? Maybe they had help!"

"This is all ridiculous assumptions!" said Helen, seeming insulted.

"Have you seen the figures wearing watches?" pressed Mr. Yatooma.

"Those were not watches," Helen protested. "They were bracelets and wrist ornaments."

"That's a load of—" Mr. Yatooma began before restraining himself. "Look, these people figured out how to count time before anyone else. They came up with the whole sixty seconds, sixty minutes thing we still use today. Split the sky into twelve parts—bam! That's where we get twelve hours. They could look at the stars and tell you exactly what was gonna happen up there. Even knew when eclipses were coming."

"Does anyone know what we call that?" I asked the students.

"Minutes and seconds," Zaya said with his signature grin.

"Yes, but what's the system called?"

Lola tilted her head in thought. "Is it like an ancient calculator?"

"The sexagesimal system," a quiet voice said from the back.

"That's right," I agreed. "They based this method on their observations of the moon and stars."

Mary retrieved her notebook from Lola and flipped to a fresh page. "We should make a list of evidence for and against Lola's theory."

"Now, now, children!" said Helen, nearly fainting. "Stop this nonsense at once!"

The group ignored her and clustered around the map, theories bouncing between them.

"Maybe we're the aliens' civilization now?" Zaya said.

"The truth is we still have much to learn about the ancient Chaldeans," I said with a wink. I pointed to an alcove where ancient figures seemed to emerge from darkness. "And some of those secrets are waiting for us there."

CHAPTER 5

Divine Shadows

The stone figures stood silent in their shadows. As we approached, their eyes seemed to follow our movement across the floor. Helen stayed a little behind.

"These deity statues tell us how the Chaldeans viewed their gods," I said, gesturing to the nearest figure. "Look at the eyes. They believed these statues could see and watch humans."

A cloud passed overhead, dimming the gallery. The stone eyes gleamed, and even Zaya fell silent.

"Creepy," Mary said, stepping back from the stone gaze.

"The Mesopotamians had this wild ceremony called 'opening the mouth,'" Mr. Yatooma said, moving beside me. "Bam! They'd bring these statues to life right there."

Zaya pushed forward. "This one's missing its nose! Did it break?"

"Many of these statues were deliberately

damaged," I explained, my voice dropping a little. "When armies invaded and conquered a city, they would often mutilate the statues of their enemies' gods."

"That's how you crushed your enemy's spirit," Mr. Yatooma punched his palm. "Smash their gods, and—"

A sharp electronic chirp cut through the gallery's hushed atmosphere. Mary fumbled with her phone, her cheeks flushing as she silenced it.

The light began to fade as we reached the edge of the Sumerian Empire exhibit. I paused at a row of small figures nearly hidden in the shadows. "Wait," I said, holding up my hand. The students clustered closer, drawn to the ancient worshippers with their folded hands and upturned faces. "There's something here you need to see before we continue." The air grew still, as if the centuries-old statues were holding their breath.

"Just like how we pray now," Helen observed softly, her earlier distress forgotten in this sacred space.

"The Sumerians were deeply faith-based people," I said, "who attributed their achievements to the highest Creator."

"Of course they did!" Mr. Yatooma's eyes lit up with pride. "Our people have always—"

Helen cleared her throat, cutting him off. As the group turned back to the statues, the shadows seemed to deepen around their ancient forms. I explained each deity's role, from healing, to justice, air, sun, and so on and so forth. The stone figures appeared to stand taller, as if listening to their names being called.

"So they had a whole team of gods?" Zaya asked.

"These weren't just decorations," I said, noticing how Lola's fingers reached out, then pulled back, as if the statues' energy had shocked her. "Berossus, a Chaldean priest who we'll meet again, wrote of them, including Tiamat, the great goddess of the sea. Her name was also Namma or Nammu—'blessing'—like my maiden name, Namou."

"You're named after a goddess?" Mary's whisper carried through the suddenly still air.

"Through my grandfather's line, yes." The words had barely left my mouth when a warm breeze—impossible in the climate-controlled gallery—swept through, carrying the tang of ancient seas. The small statues' shadows wavered, as if they were swaying.

Mary's notebook pages rustled, and Lola wrapped her arms around herself. The air grew thick with the weight of centuries.

"Berossus wrote that Tiamat and her husband Apsu created all other gods," I continued, my voice steady despite the growing energy in the room. "Gula the healer, Shamash the just, Enlil the wind-commander…"

With each name, the breeze grew stronger. The shadows cast by the statues no longer matched their forms.

"A big family tree," Zaya said.

"Each with their sacred duty," I said. "The Sumerians knew their achievements came from the divine."

"Then why did they vanish?" The question burst from Mary, her notebook clutched to her chest. "What happened to their civilization?"

"People don't just disappear," Zaya added, but his voice wavered as the nearest statue's shadow shifted again.

Lola's hand shot up with a slight tremble. "Maybe they went… home?" She pointed upward, and for a moment, the ceiling seemed to ripple like water.

The children's nervous laughter was swallowed by the heavy air. I smiled, knowing the Akkadian Empire exhibit ahead held answers deeper than they imagined. "Have you found your answers yet?" I asked.

The three students huddled closer together, their eyes darting between the statues that now seemed to watch their every move.

"Not even close," Mary whispered, her notebook pressed against her like a shield.

"Perfect," I said, leading them toward the trails of the next section of the gallery. "Because this story?" I paused, feeling the ancient power pulse around us. "It's only beginning."

PART 2

THE AKKADIANS

CHAPTER 6

Beginnings of an Empire

The Akkadian Empire awaited us. The children shuffled their feet and chattered excitedly as we moved along, their sneakers squeaking against the floor. Bordering the gallery, olive green, cobalt blue, and gold tiles caught light. Their intricate patterns drew us deeper into the past.

"Gather 'round and listen up," I said.

Soon a hush fell over the group.

"The Akkadian Empire ruled from 2350 to 2150 BC," I began.

Mary raised her hand. "That's over four thousand years ago?"

"Yes, Mary, and although we've taken only a few steps north in this exhibit, the Akkadian cities were actually far to the north of Sumer."

"Who ruled during this empire?" Lola cut in, lifting her phone before remembering the museum rules.

Mr. Yatooma's hand rose to his chest, with his index finger pointed, as if to say, 'Excuse me.' But Helen's glance reminded him to let the students answer first.

Mary's hand then went up first, as expected, but Zaya was already calling out, "Thor, because he had a super big hammer!" He mimed swinging the legendary weapon.

Lola's eyes lit up. "Queen Elsa from Frozen!" She threw her arms forward in a dramatic flourish, as if casting ice magic.

"The Rock!" someone added. "Have you seen those Akkadian statues? They're totally buff!"

While my gentle smile encouraged the creative responses, I noticed that Helen's eyebrows climbed higher with each suggestion.

"My uncle Steve," Lola dreamed up. "He tells everyone he rules everything anyway."

I pressed my lips together, fighting back laughter.

"Cleopatra's pet cat!" a girl called out, her arms bent in an exaggerated hieroglyph pose.

Mary's pencil flew across her notebook, determined to record every suggestion.

"Actually," Mr. Yatooma began, his booming voice filling the room, "the Akkadian Empire was one of the most significant early civilizations. They created this incredible system of roads and trade routes, though probably not quite Wonder Woman level," he added with a wink.

"Those are creative guesses," I said, redirecting their attention. "But let's save the superheroes for movie night." I moved toward the towering statue of Sargon, its single carved eye seeming to watch our every move. "Has anyone heard of Sargon the Great?"

Mary's hand rose tentatively.

"Ah, good. Now, imagine a baby, born to a high priestess in a sacred temple." My voice dropped lower, drawing them in. "This child, whose father remained unknown, was placed in a reed basket that floated on the flowing waters. The river carried him to a humble gardener who served in the temple of Ishtar, goddess of both love and war. This gardener raised the boy, never knowing he would become the founder of an empire, a great king."

I paused, watching their faces. Even Helen's crossed arms had dropped to her sides, caught in the ancient tale. "Does this story sound familiar to anyone?"

"Moses!" Mary led the chorus of responses.

"These ancient stories show how a chosen leader can rise from humble beginnings," I said, "proving that greatness can come from the most unexpected places."

Zaya's hand went up, his eyes fixed on the statue. "Why does he only have one eye? Was he a pirate?"

"That single eye represented something special," I said. "The artists were showing that Sargon had divine wisdom, that he could see what others couldn't. It meant he was chosen by the gods to rule."

Mr. Yatooma cleared his throat, ready to share more historical information, but Helen's warning glance kept him in check…for the moment, at least.

"So you're saying these stories are even older than the Bible?" Mary asked.

Mr. Yatooma could no longer contain himself. "Listen, sorry to interrupt, but you guys need to hear about George Smith!" He stood firm on his heels, with a relaxed stance. He looked like a diplomat from the Middle East. "George was this regular engraver, nothing special, but he taught himself all these dead languages because he was just that obsessed. The British Museum people were like, whoa, this guy's got skills, and hired him!"

Helen opened her mouth to protest, then closed it, caught up despite herself in his enthusiasm.

"So check this out," Mr. Yatooma continued, his hands flying everywhere. "He's going through thousands of these crusty old tablets, and bam!"—making Mary and Lola jump—"he finds this epic story about Gilgamesh! But here's the best part." He leaned forward conspiratorially. "When he figured out it had basically the same flood story as Noah's Ark, he got so excited that he started strippin' off his clothes and dancing around the museum like a maniac!"

The children roared with laughter.

"That's not exactly how we'd phrase it in academic circles," I explained, though I couldn't help smiling at his infectious enthusiasm.

"Did he really get that excited in the museum?" Zaya asked.

"Of course!" Mr. Yatooma beamed. "Imagine a proper Victorian gentleman so thrilled about ancient tablets that he forgot all about being proper! You see, Gilgamesh was this legendary king, two-thirds god and one-third human. He went on incredible quests, fought monsters, and searched for immortality. It's like an ancient superhero story, but with deep questions about... well, everything!"

He leaned sideways. "And get this—there's this beast-man named Enkidu who lives wild with gazelles and stuff, until this temple lady civilizes him. Then bam!"—more jumps from the children—"he and Gilgamesh become best friends after this epic wrestling match! It's like WWE meets philosophy!"

"Wrestling?" a kid in the back asked.

"Oh man, you don't even know! They smashed pillars and shook walls! But that's not even the craziest part. See, there's this giant named Humbaba who—"

Helen finally stepped in. "Let's let our guide continue."

"Thank you, Mr. Yatooma, for this delightful information," I said and pointed to a book titled *The Chaldean Account of Genesis* set next to ancient tablets. "George Smith published this book in 1876, after discovering and translating these ancient clay tablets. In it, he shows how stories like the Great Flood existed in Mesopotamian literature long before they appeared in the Bible. While we can't date some of these tablets precisely before 2000 BC, we know these epic tales were being told and carved into clay long before that. It's like finding the first draft of history itself."

The children pressed closer to the display case. Lola's nose nearly touched the glass as she squinted at the cuneiform writing. The tiny wedge-shaped marks caught the light oddly, seeming to pulse like a heartbeat. For a moment, I could have sworn that I saw fingerprints pressed into the clay—not ancient ones, but fresh, as if the scribe had just stepped away.

"Wait, who's Uruk?" Mary asked, reading the label beneath the tablet.

"Is that like *irook*?" Zaya said, his grin returning.

Several students, including Mary, giggled. "It's pronounced *ee'roog*, not *irook*!" she called out.

Their laughter pulled me back to the present. "Well, Uruk is something completely different," I said, straightening my jacket. "It was one of the most important ancient cities in Mesopotamia."

"But what's *ee'roog*?" a non-Chaldean student asked, looking confused.

"They're Iraqi food patties," I said.

"Oh! Were they named after the city of Uruk?" Mary asked, her pencil poised to record the connection.

"Let's save our food discussion for lunch," said Helen, then whispered in my ear. "Can you give me that recipe later?"

I nodded. "Children, listen up. We have an even more fascinating story to explore, King Sargon. He conquered Sumer around 2334 BCE and created the Akkadian Empire, changing everything in ancient Mesopotamia. Ready for some surprising facts?"

The kids leaned forward. Mary flipped to a fresh page in her notebook.

"Imagine someone so powerful they united all the independent cities under one rule," I said. "Before Sargon, each city had its own ruler, its own laws, even its own way of measuring grain and gold. He standardized everything, from the weight of silver used in trade to the size of bricks used in buildings. It would be as if someone combined all your different schools into one super school, with the same textbooks and same rules."

"Just as powerful as the Avengers," Zaya whispered excitedly.

"In a way," I said with a smile. "In the markets of Akkad, you might hear five different languages being spoken. Traders from India brought peacocks and spices, while merchants from modern-day Afghanistan brought deep blue lapis lazuli for jewelry. Their scribes created the world's first dictionary, translating Sumerian words into Akkadian. They had an incredible system to manage all this trade."

"So they were the first Amazon delivery?" Zaya called out.

"More of an ancient DoorDash," another boy said, and the boys high-fived each other, grinning.

"You're not far off," I said. "They even created what we might call the world's first postal service. Look at this tablet here. See these markings around the edge? That's a clay envelope. Inside, there might be anything from a love letter to a receipt for twenty goats. Each envelope was sealed with the sender's personal stamp. We've found some with beautiful carvings of lions and bulls."

"That's awesome!" said Lola.

"More than a receipt for twenty goats," I continued, turning the tablet carefully in my hands, "this particular message tells us about a festival where dancers from seven different cities performed together. Before Sargon, these cities might have been fighting each other. Now they were sharing their music and dances."

"Wow," breathed Lola, "like an ancient talent show!"

The children's excitement filled the gallery, but something even more remarkable awaited them. I touched the ancient tablet before us, feeling its connection to someone who had changed history forever.

CHAPTER 7

First Signature

"The most incredible part of Sargon's story might be his daughter, Enheduanna," I said.

"Who was she?" Mary asked, her eyes bright at the mention of a powerful woman.

"She was a princess, a high priestess, and, get this, the first writer in recorded history. Not male or female, but the first writer in recorded history," I stressed.

The room fell quiet. Mr. Yatooma leaned back, visibly impressed. Helen straightened her glasses.

"The first writer ever was a girl?" Lola's voice rose in pitch.

"And she came from our ancestors?" Mary gripped her pencil tight.

"The first to sign her name," I said. "Other scribes wrote before her, but tradition was that they did not sign their name. She was the first to declare 'this is mine, I wrote this.'"

"Take that, Shakespeare!" Mary punched the air.

I smiled, noting Mary's pride in her heritage, yes, but also recognition of a kindred spirit across millennia who refused to stay silent.

"What did she write about?" Lola asked.

"She wrote about and to the goddess Inanna, who she called 'Queen of all the divine powers, resplendent light.' In her poems, Inanna could make mountains bow, turn paradise to wasteland and wasteland to paradise."

A strong shaft of sunlight pierced through the high windows, revealing dust particles that swirled into impossible patterns. Mary's quick note-taking slowed as she watched the dancing light. Some things had to be experienced rather than recorded.

Every eye fixed on me.

"In her most famous poem, she writes of being thrown out during a rebellion: 'I, who once sat triumphant, have been driven forth from my temple. Like a swallow, they chased me from my window, and I must fly for my life.'"

The silence stretched, deep and complete.

"She gave us humanity's first-person writings about power," I said. "Having it, losing it, fighting to get it back."

We fell into a spell for a moment. Finally, Mary

broke the spell. "Is there a statue of her? I want to see what she looked like."

"Archaeologists found her disc in 1927." I pointed at a small artifact. "It shows her performing a ritual, surrounded by her attendants."

The metal caught the light strangely, and for a breath, the figures seemed to move within their ancient poses. Zaya, who'd been ready with another joke, fell silent. The disc's surface rippled like water, then stilled. Nobody mentioned it, but Mary's hand found Lola's arm, and they exchanged a quick, wondering glance.

Mary's pencil flew across the page as I described, "She's wearing an elaborate flounced robe that reaches to her ankles, with beautiful pleated layers that would have shimmered as she moved."

"Like a princess dress," Lola whispered, smoothing her own clothes.

"Her hair is styled in the intricate fashion of high priestesses," I continued, "arranged in waves and topped with a special headdress called a gala."

"Who are the people around her?" Mary asked.

"Her entourage," I said. "There's her personal scribe holding a tablet, her chief handmaiden adjusting her robe, and her head hairdresser who probably spent hours creating those perfect waves."

"Even back then they had hair stylists?" Zaya asked, genuinely surprised.

The question lacked his usual sarcasm. Instead, his voice held a note of discovery. It was as if the ancient world was finally becoming real to him. It was no longer just a collection of dates and names, but a place where people lived, worked, and cared about their appearance, just like today.

"Yes, and behind her stands her cupbearer," I continued, "ready to serve, and her chief temple assistant carrying ritual objects. The disc shows her performing a libation ceremony. That's a special ritual where she would pour sacred liquids as offerings to the gods."

Complete silence fell over the group, clearly absorbed in the story. Even Zaya and a few of the boys, who had been fidgeting earlier, stood transfixed.

"Her father made her high priestess as part of his plan to bring unity and peace between different people," I explained. "Enheduanna used her heartfelt poetry to help with this mission."

"Like how we try to bring people together today?" Lola asked thoughtfully.

"Yes, Lola," I said. "She believed in using her talents to make the world a better place, something we still value in Chaldean culture today."

"Did they build statues of her?" a girl asked.

I shook my head. "Surprisingly, they didn't cele-brate her achievements much back then. But today, she's becoming famous again. In fact, she's one of the heroines in my film, *Pomegranate*."

"Really?" the children exclaimed in unison.

"Yes!" I nodded. "And in my book, *Mesopotamian Goddesses*, I wrote about her and other remarkable women from ancient Iraq who helped build the Cradle of Civilization."

"Can we read your book?" Mary asked eagerly.

Helen beamed in a way she never had before. "Perhaps we could add it to the school library?" she asked, eyeing Mr. Yatooma.

"Of course!" he said with his usual enthusiasm and some students laughed, surprised as I was by Helen's out-of-character reaction. She, meanwhile, smiled proudly.

"These aren't just old stories," I concluded, giv-ing a nod of gratitude to Helen and Mr. Yatooma. "They're part of our heritage, connecting us to our Chaldean roots."

I led them to the next display, where artifacts sparkled under museum lights.

"The world's first hospitals were created in Mesopotamia," I said, and Mary's pencil paused mid-note.

"Archaeologists found evidence of hospital beds

in the ancient city of Mari, arranged in rows just like modern hospitals. They even had special healing centers called 'bit asûti' where doctors would treat patients."

I paused, touching my gold bracelets from Baghdad.

"This healing tradition never left us. My great-great grandmother Maria was known throughout her village as a powerful healer. People traveled for days to see her. She rode horses alone and owned land—a smart businesswoman too."

The children listened, attentively.

"My father Hermiz inherited this gift of healing. As a bonesetter, people came to our door with broken bones, dislocations, and torn ligaments, often choosing his methods over hospital visits." I smiled at the memory. "I remember watching him kneel beside a man on our floor cushions, gently examining his injured leg while the man groaned in pain. My mother Shamamta would carry in a tub of warm water, its steam curling around her like a shawl. She'd set it carefully beside my father with fresh towels, then bring out this special olive-green soap marked with Arabic inscriptions."

Everyone listening was mesmerized.

"What was the soap for?" Lola asked.

"That soap recipe is thousands of years old," I

said. "They say the Babylonians made it first. People used it for everything: washing, healing wounds, treating skin problems. The same wisdom, passed down through generations."

The air seemed to thicken with the scent of olive oil and herbs, though no one else appeared to notice.

"Do you have healing powers too?" she asked.

I smiled mysteriously. "We shall wait and see."

The children exchanged glances, clearly hoping for more.

CHAPTER 8

Healers in the Sacred Arts

The ancient gift of healing hung between us like incense as my attention shifted to a familiar symbol on the wall. "Speaking of healing traditions, there's something here you've all seen in doctor's offices—the caduceus, with its two snakes wrapped around a staff."

"Oh! I know that one!" Mary said. "It's on my pediatrician's wall!"

"While many think it came from Greece, its first appearance was here in ancient Mesopotamia. It belonged to Ningishzida, the god of healing and magic."

The carved snakes on the wall seemed to writhe in the shifting light. Mary blinked twice, but when she looked again, they were just ordinary carvings. She sketched a tiny snake in the margin of her notes, something the usually fact-focused girl had never done before.

"He was the son of Gula, the healing goddess," I

said. "Remember her? She sat on her throne with a loyal dog at her feet. Some say you can still hear the echo of her dog's protective bark in ancient ruins."

"That's very odd," griped Helen.

"Even goddesses need their furry friends," Lola whispered, making Zaya and Mary grin.

I guided them to a tablet carved with cuneiform script. "Now, let me tell you about someone very special. This tablet holds the story of Kubaba, the only queen listed among Sumerian kings. And her story? It begins in a tavern."

The children moved closer. The tablet's surface rippled once, like water disturbed by rain, then stilled. Several students exchanged knowing glances.

"Kubaba started as a tavern keeper—"

"You mean, the queen worked as a bartender!" Zaya's hand flew to his mouth.

"In those days, taverns were important gathering places," I said. "She ruled for a hundred years and brought such wealth to her people that they said she must have been blessed by Ninkasi herself."

"Who's Ninkasi?" the children asked in unison.

"The goddess of beer!" Mr. Yatooma burst out, earning an abstinent smile from Helen.

"Yes," I said. "Her hymn is actually the world's oldest beer recipe, written four thousand years ago. The Sumerians were the original master brewers.

Everyone received rations, even children—" I quickly added, seeing Helen's concern, "though it wasn't like modern beer. Think of it more as a nutritious grain drink."

"Still," Mary whispered to Lola, "imagine having that in your lunch box instead of milk!"

"Would you like to hear the priestesses' morning chant to Ninkasi?" I asked. "It's both a prayer and a recipe."

The children nodded eagerly, and before Helen could protest, I began:

> "Born of flowing water... perfect for the embrace of Enlil,
> Ninkasi, born of flowing water... perfect for the embrace of Enlil,
> You are the one who handles the dough with a big shovel,
> Mixing in a pit, the bappir with sweet aromatics...
>
> Ninkasi, you are the one who bakes the bappir in the big oven,
> Puts in order the piles of hulled grains,
> You are the one who waters the malt set on the ground...
> The noble dogs keep away even the potentates.

You are the one who soaks the malt in a jar,
The waves rise, the waves fall…
You are the one who spreads the cooked mash
    on large reed mats,
Coolness overcomes…

When you pour out the filtered beer of the
    collector vat,
It is like the onrush of Tigris and Euphrates!"

The words hung in the air like mist. Mary's pen had stopped moving, caught in the rhythm of the verse. When the silence broke, Lola raised her hand. "What's bappir?"

"That was their special bread made just for brewing," I said. "They would bake it until almost burnt, then crumble it into their beer mixture. The hymn was their family recipe, passed down through generations of priestesses."

"Is that why so many Chaldeans have liquor stores?" Zaya asked.

Mary shot him a look, but I smiled at the connection. "You're noting something about our community's journey. The Sumerians valued hospitality and commerce, traits that carried through generations."

Mr. Yatooma nodded at the response.

"But that's a story we'll explore in the Journey to

America gallery," I continued, "where we'll see how our ancestors adapted their business skills to their new home."

Mary wrote in her notebook while Zaya and Lola exchanged glances, maybe thinking of their own family businesses.

"But wait until you hear about Ninhursag and her paradise called Dilmun." I paused, watching them.

Mr. Yatooma shifted forward, while Helen raised her hand in a gentle "wait" gesture.

"Picture a place where ravens never cawed and lions never hunted, where peace ruled. Until her husband, Enki, couldn't resist eating the forbidden plants. Sounds familiar?"

"Like Adam and Eve!" Mary said.

"The story of Dilmun shows us how the Sumerians understood creation and healing," I continued. "When Enki falls ill from eating the plants, Ninhursag creates eight new healing deities, one for each part of his body that ached. These weren't just stories to them. They showed how women held the power of both creation and healing."

The children stood fixed in place. Lola's hands were clasped, while Zaya had stopped fidgeting. Even Mary's pencil had stilled.

Mr. Yatooma watched her students, seeing their

heritage come alive. Helen's stern expression had softened, caught up in the ancient tales.

"Now," I said, gesturing to the next gallery, "let's meet the Babylonians. Their stories are just as remarkable."

The students followed, transformed by the tales they'd heard. Mary walked tall, as if wearing Enheduanna's headdress, while clutching her notebook like a sacred tablet. Lola and Zaya stepped carefully, as if treading through Dilmun itself.

Before I could begin the next section, Mr. Yatooma seized the moment by pulling out a folded paper, his excitement palpable. His voice grew stronger as he read, "From *The Chaldean Account of Genesis*: The Babylonians saw the stars as more than markers of seasons. Like in Genesis 1:14, they believed the heavenly bodies were divine signs, their positions telling earth's story."

He tucked the paper away with a triumphant smile, clearly relishing the spotlight. "This is simplified, of course," he added, looking up. "Just as God gave monarch butterflies the ability to find their way to Mexico without a map, and just as He blessed Border Collies with the instinct to herd sheep, He blessed our people with the gift of reading the heavens! You see, being astronomers and scholars isn't just what Chaldeans did. It's who we are, deep in our bones. Our ancestors passed down this wisdom, this connection to the stars, generation after generation. It's like… how do you say… it's woven into the very fabric of who we are!"

"Star people," Lola whispered, her face shining with wonder.

The museum lights dimmed as pinpoints of light danced across the ceiling. Mary added a constellation to her notebook's margin, her precise handwriting flowing into something more artistic, as if cuneiform had worked its way into her style.

Mr. Yatooma's words hung in the starlit air. I watched the children's faces, transformed by these ancient stories flowing through their modern hearts. I then led them toward the Babylonian Empire's secrets, where even greater mysteries awaited.

PART 3

THE BABYLONIANS

CHAPTER 9

The Blending of People

We moved into the Babylonian section of the gallery. The children's footsteps echoed through the marble hall. The ancient stones seemed to whisper kind greetings as we passed. I greeted them in return, though without using words.

"We're going to witness one of history's most fascinating blending of peoples," I said, touching the gold pendant around my neck, "when Sumer and Akkad became one. Imagine mixing two different colors of paint until you can't tell where one begins and the other ends."

The children craned their necks upward at the massive Code of Laws stele that towered at 7.4 feet. The stone surface was covered in rows of cuneiform writing, and at the top, King Hammurabi stood before the sun god Shamash. Mary pulled out her notebook, which she had temporarily put away, and frantically sketched the monument. Lola stepped forward, positioning herself at the front of the group. Everyone pressed closer, like paparazzi trying to catch a glimpse of a king stepping out of his castle.

"Remember our friends, the Chaldeans, those brilliant stargazers we just learned about?" I gestured back toward the astronomy exhibit.

They nodded.

"Well, they became part of something even bigger—the mighty Babylonian Empire. The Babylonians built huge cities with broad streets and tall temples. They created maps of the stars and wrote their stories on clay tablets. And the Chaldeans weren't just good at reading the stars. They became some of the most important people in Babylon."

With a dramatic flourish, Mr. Yatooma produced a yellowed note from his pocket, his eyes twinkling with theatrical delight. "Listen to this!" he proclaimed, his voice resonating through the gallery. "'Babylon, which is the capital of the Chaldean races, long held an outstanding celebrity among the cities in the whole of the world!'" He paused for effect, scanning his captive audience. "Written by none other than Pliny the Elder himself, in his masterwork Natural History—the grandest surviving text from the Roman Empire!" He tucked the note away with the same theatrical flair he'd shown in producing it.

The children stood in awe-struck silence.

"So, let me get this straight," said Mary, studying the cuneiform intently. Her eyes moved methodically across the stone surface. "The Chaldeans became Babylonians?"

"The Chaldeans have always been great at assimilating," I explained, but before I could continue, Mr. Yatooma stepped forward, his voice booming through the gallery.

"Of course," he said, laughing, heartily. "We Chaldeans are like chameleons. We adapt, but we never lose our true colors!"

Helen crossed her arms, eyebrows raised at Mr. Yatooma's interruption, but his warm smile never wavered.

I pulled a worn notecard from my pocket. "Let me read something that might help you understand," I said. "In the 1979 *Seventh-Day Adventist Dictionary*, Chaldea is described as the land between the Tigris and Euphrates rivers where Chaldean tribes settled. After they conquered Babylonia and built their empire, the name 'Chaldea' came to mean all of Babylonia. You can see this throughout the Old Testament." I rattled off the references: "Jeremiah 50:10, 51:24, Ezra 11:24…"

I trailed off, noticing their glazed expressions.

"Picture a game of musical chairs where different groups kept taking control," I continued. "The

Akkadian Empire that Sargon built started having problems. People in different cities weren't getting along, and some wanted to rule themselves. Then, around 2100 BCE, the Sumerians came back to power. They created what we call the Ur III dynasty—a family of rulers who controlled the region from the city of Ur."

They still seemed confused, so I said, "Think of Native Americans. They're Americans, but they remember their heritage."

Their expressions finally indicated they understood the point I was trying to make.

"But then, a city called Babylon started becoming important," I said. "A king named Hammurabi came to power there. Imagine him as a teacher who gets all the students in different classrooms to follow the same rules."

"I can relate," said Zaya, most seriously. "Mr. Yatooma did this when he made us use the same homework folders."

The children laughed, and Mr. Yatooma eyed him. "Hahaha," he said.

"He brought all the separate city-states together under Babylon's leadership," I said.

"That's what some country leaders do, even today, don't they?" Mary asked.

"In my mind, these little kingdoms fit together as puzzle pieces," Lola said.

"That's a strong image," I said. "The Babylonians had a plan to expand. They looked at the Sumerians' achievements—their writing, their stories, their way of life—and preserved them while adding their own ideas."

"Like my mom's spinach stew," Lola said. "When our neighbor told her to put in scrambled eggs, it tasted better…"

"Scrambled eggs in spinach stew?" Mary asked, looking up from her notebook with a frown and sticking out her tongue. "Yuk!"

"Mamma Mia, so delicious!" Zaya jumped in, kissing his fingertips with an exaggerated Italian gesture.

"*Ma Basima!*" The clear voice rang out in Chaldean, startling everyone. It came from a blond boy who had been hovering near Zaya all afternoon, whispering and grinning but never speaking up. Until now.

The children burst into laughter, and the adults joined in.

"I see someone taught you our language," I said.

"Yeah."

"What other words do you know?" I asked him.

"Not many," he said. "They mostly taught me swear words."

As the laughter escalated, Helen's eyes narrowed. "John," she said, her voice carrying that particular tone mothers reserve for public warnings. She made the up-and-down motion with her hand—the private signal that meant a conversation waited at home. The boy shrank a little but kept his chin up, something defiant in his half-smile.

I studied them both, pieces clicking into place. His blond hair and innocent face, with small, warm eyes and a playful smile, radiated a sense of mischievousness and a neat, carefree vibe. This must be Helen's son! He'd been shadowing Zaya all this time, sharing that same glint in his eyes. His mother's stern demeanor had kept him quiet until now, when the moment, and perhaps the subject, gave him the courage to speak up.

A loud yawn broke through the gallery's hushed atmosphere. The boy who'd done it quickly covered his mouth, but not before Mr. Yatooma caught sight of him.

"Everyone, listen up!" Mr. Yatooma's voice caused quite a few to straighten up instantly. "Remember, there's an extra credit quiz tomorrow," he said. "It's especially important for those who have…uh, let's just say some catching up to do." He scanned the room as though he was a binocular in action.

To steer us back on topic, I pointed to the ancient writings, while Helen's eyebrows performed their familiar dance at Mr. Yatooma's enthusiastic outburst. "By this time, Chaldeans and Babylonians shared languages, celebrated the same festivals, and worshipped in the same temples. Father Michael Bazzi painted a vivid picture of the Chaldean tribes," I said, my voice dropping to an almost whisper, forcing the children to lean in closer. "They lived among flourishing date palms, their large herds of horses and cattle dotting the landscape. These clever traders controlled the southern routes. They transported exotic treasures—ebony dark as night, ivory smooth as silk, elephant hides tough as armor, and gold as bright as sunlight."

Their eyes grew distant, as if seeing beyond the museum walls.

"Can you imagine this?" I asked, softly, tracing an invisible path in the air. "The date palms swaying in the desert wind, and caravans stretching across the horizon, loaded with their precious cargo…"

"I want to go there," said Lola, dreamily.

"You got it," said Mr. Yatooma, and he snapped his fingers. "Carriage…Come here at once and take us to…" He stopped and stared at me guessingly. "Where are we exactly?"

"We're at the Babylonian Empire," I said, playing along. "Just drive through the gates of Babylon. You can't miss it, the most magnificent city in all of Mesopotamia, with its hanging gardens reaching toward the sky."

"All aboard!" Mr. Yatooma called out, pretending to hold reins. He guided our imaginary carriage through the ancient streets. "Whoa there!" he called out suddenly, pulling back on his invisible reins. "Look what we have here—right in front of us stands one of the most important monuments in human history."

The children's eyes followed his gesture to the massive stele before them. The moment of playful imagination had captured their attention perfectly, making them more receptive to the serious discussion ahead.

"Chaldeans' organization was tribal," I continued, watching the children's renewed attention with satisfaction, "and each household answered to the Sheikh, a father figure, but for an entire community."

"But Ms. Weam," said Zaya, "some people say that the Chaldeans of the Babylonian Empire are not the same as the ones who came from ancient Mesopotamia?"

"And what has led to their conclusion?" I asked.

"Some say that there isn't enough evidence to support that idea," Mary said.

"There's plenty of evidence!" Mr. Yatooma replied, his tone defensive. "But unfortunately, you can't teach fish how to climb trees."

"What does that mean?" the children asked, confused.

"Listen," he said, leaning forward, his voice firm. "Some people want to disprove something just because it's hard to see. The Hebrews referred to Babylonians as 'Chaldeans' in the Bible. Do you think they chose that name randomly in such an important book? This name didn't just happen by chance; it shows how the Hebrews understood their world. It also didn't survive by mere coincidence."

"Exactly," I said, easing the tension in the room. "The Chaldeans never disappeared. They merged into something greater, like a stream joining a river. Their knowledge of stars, mathematics, and medicine became part of Babylonian achievement—not lost, but transformed."

I gestured toward another gallery. "Later, you'll see Maria Theresa Asmar's memoir. Though titled 'Babylonian Princess,' inside she wrote of her true identity as Chaldean. The world knew Babylon, but she knew who she was."

The gallery grew quieter and quieter.

The tension having settled down, I added, "And Mr. Yatooma, your passion for this history shows how deeply connected you are to it. That connection matters."

Mr. Yatooma's chest swelled. Specks of dust swirled in the light like tiny stars charting ancient trade routes. Helen's eyes tracked their path, her skepticism giving way to curiosity.

CHAPTER 10

Hammurabi's Law

As I moved to toward the next display, I watched the students' faces as history shifted before them from distant facts into a living story of human connection. "let's talk about one of the most famous rulers of this period, King Hammurabi."

"King Ham-mooooo-rabbi?" Zaya asked, making cow sounds that set off laughter.

"Ham-mu-rabi," I corrected, while Mr. Yatooma fought a smile.

"Was he a Rabbi?" Zaya asked, his eyes bright.

"No, he was not a Rabbi," I said.

Mr. Yatooma's laugh filled the gallery.

"Hammurabi created a Code of Laws and placed them here," I explained, pointing at the stele. "The purpose of the laws was to create justice, destroy evil, and to enhance the welfare of the people."

"Did he come up with all these laws?" asked Lola.

"No, but before this, the laws were scattered

across town, with people arguing over different versions. Hammurabi put a stop to the bickering by carving this massive stele with 282 laws, all organized into specific sections. In a way, it was like the world's first book!"

Mary's pencil raced across her paper, her eyes bright with understanding. "With chapters and headings!"

"That's right, Mary." I pulled out my phone, holding it up. "See how we check laws now? On phones or in books so light we can carry them in our pockets or backpacks. But this stele?" I gestured toward the replica. "It weighs tons, literally tons…"

"I bet I can lift it!" John announced, already wrapping his arms around the massive stone.

"John!" Helen's voice cracked like a whip, but it was too late. Like moths to a flame, the other boys swarmed the stele, grunting and straining in mock effort.

Mr. Yatooma and Helen restored order with stern looks and by grabbing some of the children's arms. When the giggling finally subsided, I cleared my throat. "Now, as I was saying. They placed this stele in the center of town, and people had to come to it. Whether you needed to know about divorce, trade, or theft—all of life's rules were carved right here, permanent and public."

Helen uncrossed her arms. "Is this the real one from ancient times?"

"No, this is a copy from the Louvre Museum in Paris. The original is there."

"Where was it before Paris?" Mary asked, studying the monument.

"Ah, now there's a story!" I said. "A French engineer named Jacques de Morgan found it in 1901, not in Babylon but in ancient Susa, modern-day Iran. The Elamites had stolen it."

"Stolen?" several voices came in.

"They tried to erase parts to write their own story," I said.

Mr. Yatooma shook his head. "But most survived," he said.

I directed their attention upward. "See those two figures? That's Hammurabi standing before Shamash, the sun god. The stone is diorite, a beautiful gray rock."

"What language are all these little marks?" Mary traced the air with her finger.

"That's Akkadian," I said. "An ancestor of Aramaic."

As the children looked with awe, Mr. Yatooma stepped forward, ready to provide additional notes. "Ha! You think that's impressive? Let me tell you something! Even after the Akkadians took over, the kings had to keep using Sumerian for all the important stuff—laws, religious texts, everything. But after this dynasty—these rulers called Isin—took charge around 2000 BC?" He made a dismissive gesture. "Poof! The Sumerian language was gone, never to be seen again."

"Really?" asked Helen.

"Yes, Ma'am! Trust me, I know these things."

"What were in those laws?" someone asked.

"Well, one famous law that I'm sure you've all heard of is an 'eye for an eye, tooth for a tooth.'"

The children winced. Zaya clutched his eye dramatically, while Mary scribbled faster in her notebook. Lola took a small step back.

"Those were different times," Mr. Yatooma said gently, his warm smile reassuring the students.

"Besides laws, Hammurabi did something else clever," I said, reaching into my teaching bag. I held up two measuring cups. "He standardized weights and measures throughout his empire. The mina for weight, the cubit for length—imagine if every merchant used different sizes to measure grain or oil. These standards made trade fair for everyone."

Mr. Yatooma stepped forward. "We Chaldeans were known for our precise measurements in astronomy too!"

"They invented the shekel too," I said. "No more trading eggs for sheep."

"Woah, ancient credit cards?" Zaya joked.

"Did they have banks?" Mary asked, still studying the stele.

"The temples acted as banks," I explained. Mr. Yatooma nodded approvingly as the students' eyes lit up with recognition.

"Back to Hammurabi's Code," I gestured to the stele. "These laws introduced something we still use, innocent until proven guilty."

"That was progressive for their time," Helen remarked.

"In some ways, yes," I said. "While this empire flourished, it wasn't the end of the story." I glanced toward the next gallery. "Soon, another group would rise to power—warriors who would build their empire not through laws and trade, but through iron and fire…"

PART 4

THE ASSYRIANS

CHAPTER 11

The Mighty Assyrians

The usual echoes of footsteps and whispers slowly faded as we stepped into the new space that featured old-aged weapons. Bronze spearheads, iron swords, and siege equipment replicas lined the displays.

"This is the Assyrian gallery," I said, my footsteps the last to stop. "On the upper Tigris lies the ancient city of Assur which was the heart of the Assyrian Empire. She was the superpower of her day!"

"That she was!" Mr. Yatooma jumped in, practically shoving his way to the front. "Nineveh was so huge, it took three days just to walk around it! These people didn't mess around—best chariots in the world, food you wouldn't believe, business deals happening left and right! For three hundred years, nobody could touch them. Nobody!"

"The Assyrians were a Semitic people who lived in the upper Tigris," I said. "They built one of the world's most powerful military empires."

"They were master warriors…" Mr. Yatooma began.

"And empire builders," I added.

"Incredible organizers too," he said.

It felt like we were playing a game of who-knows-what about the Assyrians.

"Those weapons look scary," Lola whispered, inching closer to Mary as she peered at an array of arrowheads.

"One of their greatest kings was Ashurbanipal," I said, moving attention away from the weaponry. "Unlike most people of his time, he could read and write. And he did something remarkable. He built the world's first great libraries in his capital city of Nineveh."

"Was it bigger than our school library?" John called out with his newfound voice.

I reached into my teaching bag, and through the rustling, pulled out a tablet replica. "Much bigger. Imagine thousands upon thousands of clay tablets like this…"

"Over thirty thousand to be exact," Mr. Yatooma interrupted.

"Thank you, Mr. Yatooma," I said, biting my lip. He was clearly enjoying this back-and-forth. "The Assyrians created something we still use today, a library catalog system. They organized tablets by subject: medicine, astronomy, mathematics, literature, religious texts, even cooking recipes."

"Did you know that the first recipe was found from ancient Mesopotamia?" he asked. "The tablets are at the Yale Peabody Museum. You see, we Chaldeans are innovators! We don't just adapt—we improve, even when it comes to cooking." His smile was wide as he gestured as if presenting a culinary masterpiece.

"This all sounds just like our library," Mary said, dreamily.

"So, they invented the library?" Zaya groaned. "They ought to be punished for that!"

The class erupted in laughter. Even Helen's "shh" couldn't quite mask her amusement.

I pressed on, straight-faced. "If you wanted to find information about treating a sick person, you'd go to the medical section. If you needed to know about the stars, you'd check the astronomy section. They even had little clay tags, like modern library cards, to help find specific tablets."

John's hand went up again, confidence growing. "Did they have comic books?" Zaya gave him a fist-pump and asked, "How about anime?" And Mary, surprising everyone with her playfulness, added, "What about manga?"

Further ripples of laughter broke into the

museum. John beamed, now fully part of the group's easy camaraderie.

"I'm sure they had all kinds of stories, but with different names," I said. "As you might've figured out by now, they switched names up quite a bit."

My expression grew serious as my gaze drifted to the military displays. "Let's now discuss the two Assyrian princess who were brothers."

CHAPTER 12

Brothers and Empires

"When the Assyrians forced out the Babylonian king Merodach-Baladan, they tried something unusual," I said. "Their King, Esarhaddon, put two of his sons in charge. Assurbanipal ruled Assyria, while his older brother Shamash-Shuma-Ukin, nicknamed Chaldo by the Babylonians, governed Babylon. But having brothers rule these rival kingdoms didn't bring peace. During a rebellion, Chaldo made a dramatic choice. He threw himself into the flames of his burning palace rather than surrender to his younger brother."

The children gasped at this story.

"Therefore, Assurbanipal gained complete control of the Assyrian Empire in 648 BC."

"That's sad," someone said.

"Yes, it is," I continued, my tone sober. "Mesopotamia saw wave after wave of different rulers—Assyrians, Chaldeans, Babylonians—each trying to claim the land as their own. Peace was rare in those times." The air in the gallery grew heavier. Even Zaya, our perpetual motion machine, stood still.

"Four thousand years later," Mr. Yatooma said quietly, "and that part of the world still struggles to find peace."

A heavy silence fell over the group. Then Mary, ever the careful student, raised her hand as if trying to steer us back to safer ground. "Ms. Weam, who was the first to write about the Chaldeans?"

Grateful for her question, I explained, "Interestingly, we learn a lot from records left by their rivals. The first historical mention of Chaldeans appears in records from the Assyrian King Shalmaneser III, around 850 BC."

"What does 'historical mention' mean?"

"Good question," I said. "It means actual objects from that time, clay tablets with writing, royal inscriptions carved in stone. Things archaeologists can dig up and study."

"So…" Zaya furrowed his brow. "What about the Bible? It talks about Chaldeans too, right? Is that not historical?"

"The Bible does mention 'Ur of the Chaldeans' as Abraham's birthplace, which would be much earlier than 850 BC," I said. "Both biblical and archaeological sources help us understand the past, but historians tend to look for physical evidence objects and writings from the actual time period—to confirm dates and events."

"What happened next?" Mary asked anxiously.

"Oh, well, the Assyrians had a policy of deporting conquered peoples to different parts of their empire," I said, returning to the story. "Many Chaldeans and Babylonians were forced to leave their homes."

"That's what happened to my Jewish grandmother in Poland," one girl said.

"Through wars and conflict, many people's ancestors had to leave their home," I said.

"Like the Armenians too," Mary said thoughtfully.

"And the Irish during the potato famine," added Helen. "And the Greeks during the Ottoman Empire. It's part of so many family stories—even today, unfortunately."

There was a moment of silence before I continued, changing the energy from somber to lively once again. "The Assyrians were organized into clans, each following a hereditary chief. And like many groups who conquered Mesopotamia, they adopted much of Babylonian culture—everything from marriage customs to property laws."

"What made them different from the Babylonians?" asked Lola.

"Mainly their chief god," I said. "The Assyrians worshipped Asshur, while the Babylonians followed

Marduk. Both civilizations were influential in ancient Mesopotamia, but they had distinct religious practices and cultural identities. Otherwise, they lived in similar ways, farming wheat and barley, raising livestock, and building clay houses."

"Is Assyria and Ashur the same word?" asked Mary.

"Yes, and it was named after the deity Ashur, also known as Assur, their chief god."

"So were the people named after the city or after their god?" Lola asked.

"Over time, the name of the city and the god became synonymous with the people and their empire," I said. "So, while Ashur was an important figure in Assyrian culture, the name Assyrian derives from the city rather than a specific king."

"Yes, and the city of Ashur was the capital of the ancient Assyrian Empire," said Mr. Yatooma.

"What was it called before it became Assyria?" asked Helen.

"The region was known as Akkad and included other parts of ancient Mesopotamia, which featured various city-states and cultures, such as Sumer."

"Wow, all the different empires were connected like a train," said Zaya.

"That's a great comparison," I replied. "Trains have different cargos and passengers, but they're all linked together. When one part tries to cut itself off from the rest, the whole train risks falling apart and not reaching its destination. It's the same with our heritage. Every piece matters for the strength of the whole. If we ignore or fight against our shared history, we end up with a jumbled identity that's just set up for disaster."

Everyone looked at me with understanding in their eyes.

I gestured to the massive stone guardian figure. "Now, let's talk about art! The Assyrians had a unique artistic style, especially in their amazing sculptures. Check out this lamassu—a protective spirit with the head of a human, the body of a bull, and the wings of an eagle. They carved these incredible beings to guard their palace gates. If you look closely, you'll see it has five legs instead of four. This clever trick makes it look still when viewed from the front, but like it's walking when seen from the side."

"Five legs?" Zaya circled the statue. "That's some ancient special effects right there!"

"The Assyrians built the most impressive palaces," one of the boys claimed out of nowhere it seemed. "My dad showed me pictures—"

"But the Babylonians had the Hanging Gardens!" a girl from the back countered. "Everyone knows that was the most amazing—"

"Maybe," Zaya suggested thoughtfully, "each empire was impressive in its own way?"

I smiled at his mediation. "That's a mature way to look at it. In fact, both empires created architectural wonders that influenced building styles for centuries. The Assyrians were known for their massive palace complexes with these guardian figures, while the Babylonians created the legendary Hanging Gardens and the great ziggurat temples."

"What kinds of astronomical books did they have in the library?" Mary asked, her pencil flying across her notebook.

"The Chaldean chronicles included both a succession of Babylonian kings and detailed astronomical observations," I said. "This period marked a turning point in science, when 'Chaldean' became synonymous with wisdom and astronomy."

Mr. Yatooma smashed his hands together, his eyes blazed with pride. "Over time, the Chaldeans stood mighty and unbroken while the Assyrian empire fell into shadow!"

"Thank you, Mr. Yatooma. Those are interesting details," I said, catching Helen's eye. She gave me a knowing look. "I will explain that timeline of what happened in the upcoming exhibit."

"So did the Assyrian people vanish?" asked Lola.

"No, they didn't," I said.

"They didn't?" asked Lola.

"No," I said. "You see, no one's bloodline is a hundred percent this or that. The interaction created a blending of people that still flourishes in modern communities."

"Like how my mom makes dolma with grape leaves like her Greek neighbors," Mary said.

"And everyone says '*yalla*'—'hurry up, let's go!'" added Helen with a laugh, the first time I've seen her laugh, and it made me realize that she must be Greek.

"Yes," I said. "Culture is always flowing between people, just as it did back then."

CHAPTER 13

The Empire's End

We were nearing the end of the Assyrian exhibits. I wanted to share a few final details about this remarkable empire.

"The Assyrians were the first to maintain a standing army—soldiers who served full-time."

"What was the military like before that?" Zaya asked.

"Before that, most soldiers were farmers," I said. "They only fought when needed."

"Like seasonal workers?" Lola asked.

"Yes, exactly. And these stories lived on not just in writing, but in their art. The Assyrians created detailed bas-reliefs that showed important events and achievements of their kings, making their walls come alive with history."

"What were their special inventions?" Mary asked eagerly.

"They made huge advances in metalworking," I

said. "They were among the first to widely use iron tools—not just for weapons, but for farming, building, and crafting."

"What about horses?" Zaya asked. "I saw some horse stuff in the other room."

"Good eye! They developed new kinds of protective gear," I said. "They invented better horse harnesses and saddles that made riding safer and more comfortable."

"Like seatbelts for horses?" Lola said, and Zaya snickered.

"That's actually not a bad comparison," I said. "These improvements helped merchants travel longer distances to trade goods."

Mr. Yatooma stepped in. "The Assyrians' greatest strength wasn't just their military—it was their organization and feared reputation. Many cities surrendered rather than face their armies."

Zaya's brow furrowed in thought. "What happened to the Chaldeans you mentioned earlier, who were deported? Where did they go?"

"Well, they didn't go anywhere, really," I said. "They resisted the Assyrians during the eighth and seventh centuries."

"They did?" he asked.

"Yes. Led by Nabopolassar, they allied with other groups to defeat the Assyrians. This decisive moment came in 612 BC, during the siege and destruction of Nineveh, the Assyrian capital. This marked the fall of the Assyrian Empire and the death of Assyrian King Sinsharishkun."

"Was that the final defeat?" someone asked.

"No. The final defeat came in 609 BC, at the Battle of Harran, where the remnants of the Assyrian forces, led by King Ashur-uballit II, were defeated by the Chaldeans."

Everyone waited for me to say more, but I was done. For now.

"Let's dive deeper into their story and explore how their legacy shaped the region by going to the Chaldean Empire," I said.

"Yes," said Helen. "I had enough of all this talk about fighting."

The children laughed as we moved forward. They had no idea just how personal this next chapter would become.

PART 5

THE CHALDEAN EMPIRE

CHAPTER 14

Master Builders

After a short walk, we made it to the section about the Chaldean Empire. It was near the blue walls of the Ishtar Gate and a few feet away from the Hanging Gardens.

"Why does it have two names?" Mary scribbled in her notebook.

"The Chaldeans were the people who ruled Babylon during this period," I said. "Historians often call it the Neo-Babylonian Empire—'Neo' meaning 'new'—because it rose around 626 BCE."

"Ah, 626 BC!" Mr. Yatooma raised his hands like a storyteller. "Let me take you back in time, when the Chaldeans were finally strong enough to stand up to the mighty Assyrians. Nabopolassar, a brave leader, becomes the first Chaldean king. And what does he do? He makes Babylon great again! New temples, new walls, a city that would make the gods themselves proud."

"Yes, you're right, Mr. Yatooma," I said, starting to enjoy his input because he knew what he was talking about. "During this time, the most famous ruler was Nabopolassar's son, Nebuchadnezzar II."

"Whose mother?" Zaya smirked, triggering John to snicker.

"She said brother, not mother," Mary chimed in.

"Whose another?" a boy added, laughing.

"Neb-u-chad-nez-zar," I broke down each syllable.

The children burst into laughter.

Lola, who had been trailing her fingers along the wall, stopped suddenly. "Whoa," she whispered. The sound echoed off the stone walls, and the cuneiform characters flickered to life, moving across the surface like birds taking wing. She pressed her palm flat against the wall. "It's warm," she said, wonder in her voice.

"It's quite a name, I know," I said.

"Indeed," said Helen. "But more importantly, was he Chaldean?"

"Let me be clear," Mr. Yatooma said, his face flushed. "Nebuchadnezzar was Chaldean!"

"Someone told me he never identified as a Chaldean," she responded.

"That someone is an idiot!" he said, most passionately.

"Mr. Yatooma…" I tried to intervene but unsuccessfully.

"For example, for example," he said. "If his father, King Nabopolassar, was Chaldean, then wouldn't that make his son Chaldean too?"

She did not respond.

"And why he didn't identify as a Chaldean in the tablets," he continued. "A lot could factor into that. He could've done it for political reasons… or perhaps because by then, the Chaldean identity had merged with the broader Babylonian identity. After all, we're talking about someone who ruled all of Mesopotamia. Sometimes, rulers adopt broader identities to unite their people."

"Mr. Yatooma, thank you for explaining all that, and you are correct," I said. "These reasons make sense."

"Let's move on to the guided tour," Helen said turning to me and not acknowledging him.

"Well," I said, clearing my throat. "Nebuchadnezzar ruled from 605 to 562 BCE as history's master builder."

"What did he build?" Lola's eyes glazed with visions of ancient structures.

"Many things, such as the Hanging Gardens of Babylon," I said. "One of the Seven Wonders of the Old World."

"They hung in the air?" Zaya exchanged a look with John.

"Ah, let me paint you a picture!" Mr. Yatooma spread his arms wide, his eyes twinkling. "Imagine stepping into paradise itself. Layer upon layer of gardens climbing to the heavens, like our mountains back home in the old country. And the clever part? They had what we'd call the world's first water elevator! The Euphrates River's water, pushed up through giant screws, bringing life to every level."

"A water elevator?" Lola's voice rang with understanding.

"The story goes that Nebuchadnezzar built it for his wife," I said, "who missed her homeland's mountains. These gardens had trees, flowers, waterfalls pouring down the terraces…"

"But Ms.," Mary broke her silence. "How do we know this is true after thousands of years?"

"Good question," I said. "Long-ago writers left detailed accounts of the Hanging Gardens. Remember Borassus? He was a Chaldean priest who wrote about them around 290 BCE."

"Yeah, but I heard he wasn't all there, if you know what I mean," Zaya said, making a circular gesture near his temple.

"That depends on who you ask," I said.

"If you ask the extraterrestrials, they might find

him quite normal," said Lola, and her classmates chuckled.

"Greek historians like Diodorus Siculus and Strabo also documented the Hanging Gardens," said Helen, surprising us. She is Greek, I thought!

"Literally!" Zaya said with thumbs up.

"But did they actually see them?" Mary's pen scratched across her notebook.

"No," I replied. "They based their writings on earlier accounts. Philo of Byzantium gave the most detailed description in his Seven Wonders of the World."

"Philo?" John asked, crinkling his nose. "Is that short for Philosopher?"

Others took turns saying "Byzantium" like it was a magical spell.

"What if they just made it up?" Mary challenged this theory and Lola nodded beside her.

Mr. Yatooma drew himself up, his stance like a tiger readying to defend its territory, when I came to the rescue. "Well, archaeologists found evidence that matches these writings. They uncovered foundations of a massive building with thick walls that were strong enough to support garden terraces. They even discovered the wells and water system described in the ancient texts."

"Ancient pipes?" Mary asked.

"They found remains of what's called an Archimedes screw," I said. "It's like a giant corkscrew that lifted water to the higher levels. The Babylonians were brilliant engineers."

The children leaned forward. Lola edged closer, while Zaya watched intently from his corner.

"What makes archaeology so exciting is that we're still uncovering ancient mysteries," I said, gesturing to the blue-tiled wall. "This is a reproduction of the Ishtar Gate—Babylon's grand entrance, discovered by archaeologists."

CHAPTER 15

The Gates of Blue

"That's a pretty blue." Lola touched the blue tiles.

"The blue comes from lapis lazuli, a semi-precious stone," I said. "Here's the twist—this stone didn't exist in Mesopotamia."

"Where was it from?" Mary's notes filled her page.

Mr. Yatooma stepped forward, tail-tip twitching with anticipation. "Ah! They traveled thousands of miles to get it. All the way to what is now Afghanistan. They organized trade routes across mountains, deserts, and hostile territories for this blue stone!"

"That's far!" Zaya turned to John. "Why not use local stones?"

"Nothing else created this particular brilliant blue color," I said as Helen watched with narrowed eyes. "Like gold, which they imported, the Mesopotamians went to extremes for what they wanted."

Lola raised her hand. "How did they plan such long trips with no phones, no GPS?"

"Remember, historians have a theory," I lowered my voice.

"Aliens?!" John and Zaya slapped hands.

"Children today," Mr. Yatooma began, shaking his head in disbelief. "Sometimes I wonder how you all survive without Google!"

The children stared at him in mock horror, then burst out laughing. Mr. Yatooma raised his arms, exasperated, as if to say, "Well, I tried," ready to give up, before he changed his mind. "But listen," he said, "these inventors and creators—and I mean our ancestors, all of humanity's ancestors—achieved the unthinkable without modern technology. Can you imagine? They navigated the world with nothing but their wits and a bit of courage. Get it?"

The children fell silent, their faces glowing with wonder as they imagined a world where people crossed deserts and mountains just to find the perfect shade of blue.

"The same brilliant blue that they traveled so far to obtain was used throughout the gate," I said. "This blue, along with golden-yellow glazed bricks, formed images of dragons, bulls, and lions. Imagine walking through this gate—about 38 feet high, like a four-story building! The dragons on the Ishtar Gate are about 13 feet tall, and the bulls are a little smaller, around 11.5 feet tall—a little taller than me."

The children laughed.

"Just kidding. About the height of a school bus."

"Did they think the animals were real?" Mary asked, her pen never leaving her notebook.

"Well, the lions were definitely real—they lived in Mesopotamia back then," I said. "Ancient kings even kept them in special hunting parks. The bulls were aurochs—huge wild cattle that existed then but are extinct now. But my favorite is the mushuššu dragon."

"The what dragon?" someone asked.

"Mishmash?" Zaya asked.

"Or did you mean *mishmish*?" Lola said a word that meant apricot in her mother tongue.

"The mushuššu," I repeated, nicely, though they were trying my patience by now. "It had a scaly body like a dragon, the head and front legs of a lion, the back legs of an eagle, and a snake's neck!"

"It sounds beautiful…" Mary's eyes glazed over.

"It was the sacred symbol of Marduk, the chief god of Babylon," I said and pointed to the gate. "See how the lions seem to be walking? The Babylonians created this amazing optical illusion. But these animals weren't just for decoration. Can anyone guess why they were really there?"

"To honor their gods?" Mary suggested.

"To make the city look important?" Lola tried.

"Good guesses, but no—it was something very practical," I said.

More guesses flew around the room until I held up my hand. "They were for protection. At night, with torch light flickering against the glazed bricks, these fierce creatures would seem to come alive. Imagine being an enemy approaching Babylon in the darkness, seeing these massive glowing beasts moving on the walls. Would you still want to attack?"

The children's eyes widened as they pictured it.

"That's brilliant! Just brilliant!" Lola said, dreamily.

"Ancient animation," Zaya observed, "but also ancient security system."

"I have a question," Mary said, snapping out of her reverie. "Were the dragons real?"

"The dragons weren't, but they were sacred symbols," I said. "The bulls and lions represented powerful gods."

"Speaking of sacred things," Mr. Yatooma chimed in, "did you know that many scholars think the biblical Garden of Eden was located in this region?"

"Wait—The Garden of Eden?" Lola straightened up. "The one from Sunday school?"

"That's right! The Bible describes it as being

where four rivers meet, and two of them are the Tigris and Euphrates, the same rivers that Ms. Weam has been talking about all day." He looked at me. "Isn't that so?"

"It is," I said. "The Babylonians also had their own sacred gardens, which might have inspired the story."

"Their version of Disney World," Zaya said, earning a high-five from John. "With all the fancy decorations and special events?"

"Except, instead of roller coasters, they had towering gardens and magnificent processions," I said. "You know, parts of the real Ishtar Gate still exist today in a museum in Berlin. They had to rebuild the museum around it because it was too big to fit through the doors."

"Can I tell them about the New Year's festival, Akitu?" asked Mr. Yatooma, and before I could respond, he gave himself permission. "During this time, the king would walk through this gate in a huge parade. The whole city would celebrate for eleven days!"

"Eleven days of partying?" Zaya's eyes lit up. "That beats our two-day weekend."

CHAPTER 16

The Great Exchange

"Let's not forget," said Helen, arms crossed. "There was conflicts during this golden age."

"You're referring to 597 BCE," I said, "when Nebuchadnezzar II conquered Jerusalem?"

"Indeed! And began what's known as the Babylonian Exile."

"What's an exile?" Lola asked.

"It means being forced to leave your homeland," I said. "You're absolutely right, Helen. Nebuchadnezzar brought many Jewish people from Jerusalem to Babylon. But here's where it gets interesting…"

"Did he torture them?" Zaya interrupted.

Mr. Yatooma jumped in, his chest puffed with pride. "No! While some biblical passages portray the Chaldeans negatively, consider who wrote the Old Testament."

"Who?" several kids asked, excited.

"The Hebrews!"

"Ms. Weam, is that true?" Mary asked.

"Of course it is!" Mr. Yatooma replied, slightly insulted that his expertise was being questioned.

"Well, let's look at things from an archaeological perspective," I said gently. "In 2015, they discovered about 100 clay tablets that revealed something fascinating. The Hebrew people in Babylon weren't slaves at all—they were merchants, traders, and royal officials. Some even became quite wealthy!"

"So, they just… moved in and got rich?" Helen's skepticism returned full force.

"But why kidnap them just to give them good jobs?" Zaya's voice carried unexpected weight.

"Nebuchadnezzar was very strategic," I explained. "He specifically chose educated people, skilled craftsmen, and promising young nobles. He wanted their knowledge and talents to help build his empire."

"Oh, like when all the tech companies steal each other's employees," Lola said, proud of making the connection.

"That's a very clever comparison," I nodded. "He brought scholars, priests, craftsmen, and administrators—people who could read and write, who knew about architecture, trade, and government. He even had their children educated in Babylonian schools."

"Hold up," Zaya raised his hand. "You're

telling me he conquered them… just to give them scholarships?"

"So, he was like an ancient headhunter?" Mary's pen paused mid-sentence. I noticed she'd been sketching dragons.

"But wasn't that mean, taking them from their homes?" Lola asked.

"It was definitely forced relocation," I acknowledged. "But Nebuchadnezzar knew something important—if you want to build a great empire, you need talented people. Instead of just conquering and enslaving them, he integrated them into Babylonian society. The Jewish people were allowed to keep their own communities, practice their religion, and even become wealthy merchants and royal advisors."

"And this wasn't just a Babylonian thing!" Mr. Yatooma exclaimed. "All the great empires did this—the Persians, the Romans—they weren't just conquering territories, they were collecting the brightest minds and most skilled artisans from every corner of their known world. It was like building the ultimate dream team!"

"That's an interesting way to think about it," I said. "But this practice of empire-building changed with the later Chaldeans. They became more focused on astronomy, mathematics, and religious studies. In fact, as I mentioned before, the word 'Chaldean' eventually came to mean 'astronomer' or 'scholar' or 'wisdom' rather than 'conqueror.'"

"So they went from being wise men to scientists?" asked Lola.

"Excuse you," said Mary, clearing her throat. "Wise men and wise women."

Everyone smiled.

"Yes, they found different ways to make their mark on history. Instead of building empires, they built knowledge and peaceful societies that we still use today, especially in astronomy and mathematics. But let's return to their empire for a moment. In the end, when Cyrus the Great of Persia conquered Babylon in 539 BCE and allowed them to return to Jerusalem, many chose to stay."

"Why didn't they want to go home when they could?" asked Mary.

"Well, imagine your grandparents moved to a new country , not by choice, but then you were born there. You grew up there, your business is there, your friends are there. Would you want to leave?"

The students shook their heads.

"Plus," I continued, "many saw Mesopotamia as doubly sacred. It was now their home, but it was also where Abraham, their patriarch, had come from—specifically, from the city of Ur, land of the Chaldeans. They had built synagogues, schools, and successful businesses. Some families had lived there for three generations by the time Cyrus gave them the choice to return."

"Did anyone go back?" asked Mary.

"Yes, some did return to rebuild Jerusalem. But many stayed in Babylon, creating what historians call the first major Jewish diaspora, or community living outside their homeland. They even established famous schools of learning that produced some of Judaism's most important texts."

"So Nebuchadnezzar's plan worked?" asked Zaya.

"In ways he probably didn't expect! By bringing talented people to Babylon and providing them opportunities, he inadvertently fostered a rich multicultural society that lasted long after his empire fell."

"Did they forget about Jerusalem?" Lola asked.

"Not at all. During this time, in the fifth century AD," I said, "a great synod of Jewish scholars at Sura, Babylonia, wrote important religious texts, including parts of the Talmud—their book of law and tradition."

"How big is the book?" Mary asked.

"The Babylonian Talmud is sixty-three books."

I heard gasps.

"Yes, that's quite a bit of books," I said. "So you see, they kept their faith while adopting the local language, Aramaic, which was derived from Akkadian."

"Like learning a new language in a new country?" suggested Zaya.

"Exactly!"

"What were some of these teachings?" Mary asked in a journalistic manner.

"It varied," I responded. "From fasting rituals to how one should dance before a bride."

The children giggled.

"Now, let's look at some important people during this time. Does anyone know the story of Daniel?"

Several students raised their hands. "The lions' den!" shouted Zaya.

"Yes, but there's more! Daniel became one of Nebuchadnezzar's most trusted advisors…"

"Wait, what's the lion's den and who's Daniel?" Lola asked.

"Daniel was one of the young Jewish nobles brought to Babylon," I explained. "He was chosen to serve in Nebuchadnezzar's court because he was smart, well-educated, and talented. But Daniel was also very devoted to his faith."

"What happened with the lions?" Mary pressed eagerly.

"Well, this happened later, under a different king named Darius. Some jealous officials tricked the king into making a law that said people could only pray to the king—no one else—for thirty days. They knew

Daniel wouldn't obey because he prayed to his God three times every day."

"Did Daniel stop praying?" asked Mary.

"Nope! He kept praying just like always, even though he knew he'd be punished. The punishment was…" I paused dramatically, "being thrown into a den of hungry lions!"

Several students gasped.

"But Daniel survived the night with the lions. When the king came to check on him the next morning, Daniel told him that God had sent an angel to shut the lions' mouths. He wasn't hurt at all!"

"Were they real lions?" Zaya asked, apparently confused.

"Yes! Remember how I mentioned earlier that Mesopotamian kings kept lions? They used them for hunting and, apparently, for punishment. But Daniel's faith and courage protected him."

"Okay, so back to the dream," I said, returning to our earlier discussion. "There's a famous story about how the king had a troubling dream…"

"Like a nightmare?" asked Lola.

"A very important nightmare. Nebuchadnezzar demanded that his wise men not only interpret the dream but first tell him what he had dreamed! Only Daniel was able to do both, and his interpretation came true. It predicted the fall of Babylon and the rise of other empires."

"Did it happen exactly like Daniel said?" asked Lola.

"It did," I said. "Nebuchadnezzar II died in 562 BC, and other rulers followed, but they could not maintain the Chaldean Empire as the center of power. Cyrus the Great ruled Persia by borrowing, adopting, and continuing the achievements of the empires before him."

"So, the Persians conquered Babylon, just like the dream predicted," Mary said, saddened.

"How did they live afterwards?" Zaya asked, also saddened.

CHAPTER 17

Legacy of Faith

"There's two sides to the story," said Mr. Yatooma. "On the one hand, the Cyrus Cylinder, biblical accounts, and Persian administrative policies show Cyrus as a kind ruler who respected Babylonian traditions and brought stability."

"There are two important perspectives to consider here," said Mr. Yatooma. "On the one hand, the Cyrus Cylinder, biblical accounts, and Persian administrative policies show Cyrus as a kind ruler who respected Babylonian traditions and brought stability."

"Yes," I agreed, "and that the new empire governed many different racial groups on the principle of equal responsibilities and rights for all people. It is said that the Persian rulers did not interfere with religion, tradition, customs, or trade, as long as the people paid their taxes and kept their peace.

Furthermore, the Persians made Aramaic the new administrative language."

"Well," Mr. Yatooma said, his hand slightly reaching up, "there's another side to this story. Not everyone was thrilled with Cyrus taking over. Some people were struggling with money, others felt he played favorites with certain religious groups, and quite a few still supported the old king Nabonidus. And you know what? Cyrus didn't really bring many Babylonians into his government, kind of left them out in the cold."

"So I'm dying to know," said Zaya. "Did the Chaldeans completely vanish?"

Helen gasped. "Oh, that's an awful word—dying!"

"To answer your question, Zaya, no, the Chaldeans endured," I replied. "In his book, *The Chaldean Exodus*, author Habib Hannona provides detailed accounts of how the Chaldeans settled in Assyria, particularly in northern Mesopotamia, following forced deportations centuries before Christianity. His research, along with that of other scholars, estimates their population at over half a million."

"Is that so?" Helen asked.

"Yes. When Christianity reached Mesopotamia, the Chaldeans embraced it while preserving their cultural identity. The next gallery illustrates how their ancient wisdom intertwined with this new faith, creating a legacy that endures today..."

"Actually," Mr. Yatooma said, leaning forward slightly, "we need to touch on something really fascinating about the Chaldeans in the Bible. You see, when the prophet Jeremiah was speaking to the people of Jerusalem, he told them something that might sound strange at first—he said that surrendering to the Chaldeans was actually God's will."

"But weren't the Chaldeans the conquerors?" Mary asked, looking baffled.

"That's exactly what makes this so interesting," Mr. Yatooma replied, warming to his subject. "According to the prophets, God had a bigger plan. The Book of Ezekiel tells us that God's glory actually moved from Jerusalem to Babylon, following his people there. These people became known as the 'Holy Remnants.'"

"What does that mean?" Zaya asked.

"Well, they were later called 'Anawim Yahweh' in the New Testament—the Poor of Yahweh. These were the people who had been purified through their time in Babylon, and they became incredibly important."

"Important how?" Helen asked.

Mr. Yatooma nodded enthusiastically. "From these very people—these Holy Remnants—came some of the most significant figures in Christian history. Zechariah, Elizabeth, even Mary, the mother of Jesus, were all considered part of this group. So you see, what looked like conquest was in fact part of a divine plan for spiritual transformation."

"So being Chaldean was...holy?" Lola ventured.

"Very much spiritual," I said. "That's why we find so many Chaldean communities embracing Christianity when it arrived in Mesopotamia. They already had this deep spiritual heritage that connected them to these biblical events."

I checked the time on my phone. "Before we move on, I'm curious—did you find what you were looking for in this gallery? Did it answer your questions?"

Mary beamed, clutching her notebook. "More than answered. I'm going to make a project about Enheduanna, the princess known as the first writer in recorded history. Can you imagine? A woman, the first known author!"

Lola twisted a strand of her hair, thinking. "I know everyone says the alien thing is crazy, but like... who knows what's really out there? God made so many amazing things. Look at all this stuff they built!"

"And the Chaldeans?" I turned to Zaya.

He grinned, gesturing around the room. "Habibi, the Chaldeans marched to Nineveh in 612 BC and the rest was history."

Everyone laughed.

"They never left, did they?" said Mary.

"They definitely endured," I said. "I mean, the proof is right here—I'm here, this museum is here, and their stories are still being told!"

The room fell quiet for a moment as the words sank in. Here was living proof of what these artifacts represented—not just ancient history in glass cases, but a heritage that breathed and evolved through generations.

I looked at the group before me: Mary's notebook nearly full, Zaya's restless energy now focused into genuine curiosity, Helen's initial resistance transformed into wonder. Even John, who had started the tour hanging back, now leaned forward eagerly with each new discovery. And Lola—she brought out a fresh new notebook and started taking notes.

I gestured toward the doorway leading to the Faith & Church gallery, where shafts of afternoon light painted ancient symbols across the floor. "Shall we see how this remarkable transformation took place?"

"Is this where we learn about how they became Christian?" Helen asked, seeming drawn to this topic.

"Yes, it is," I said.

Just then, a curious voice piped up from the back, "Will we find out whether we're part of the Holy See?"

"Follow me, and you'll soon know..."

YOUR TURN TO EXPLORE!

1. Family History Detective
   - Ask your parents or grandparents about their childhood memories
   - Create a family tree with names and photos
   - Write down a favorite family tradition

2. Language Explorer
   - Learn to write your name in Aramaic
   - Learn three words in a language you don't speak
   - Find out what languages your family members speak

3. Cultural Treasure Hunt
   - Draw a picture of something that represents your culture
   - Share a family recipe that's been passed down
   - Create a collection of items that tell your family's story

4. Museum Maker
   - Design your own mini-museum display about your family
   - Choose three objects that represent your heritage
   - Write museum-style labels for these objects

CONTINUE THE JOURNEY

Want to explore more stories about our ancient heritage and modern adventures? Here are some books you might enjoy by Weam Namou:

- Little Baghdad
- Pomegranate
- Mesopotamian Goddesses
- Iraqi American Series: The Lives of the Artists

You can find these books on Amazon, or visit www.weamnamou.com to discover more stories!

Other Great Books About Chaldean History and Culture:

Visit your local library or bookstore to discover more wonderful books about Chaldean history and culture! You can also ask your teachers and family members to help you find age-appropriate books about our rich heritage.

ABOUT ME, YOUR MUSEUM GUIDE AND CHALDEAN STORYTELLER!

I was born in Baghdad, Iraq as a Chaldean—we're Christian Catholics also known as Neo-Babylonians, and yes, we still speak Aramaic, the language Jesus spoke! When I was your age, just ten years old, my family and I moved to Michigan in the United States. Did you know Michigan has the largest population of Chaldeans in the whole world?

People call me the Chaldean Storyteller because I've been writing stories for almost as long as I can remember. Stories help us understand who we are and where we came from, and I've written nearly two dozen books so far! I've also made two movies that have won over forty awards. Sometimes I still can't believe that the little girl who moved from Baghdad grew up to tell stories that people all around the world want to hear.

I speak three languages—English, Arabic, and Aramaic—and I love to travel and learn about different cultures. I studied writing in college and even learned poetry in a beautiful city called Prague! When I'm not writing or working at the museum, I'm spending time with my two beautiful children, my husband, and our lovable dog who always makes us laugh.

In 2019, I began my most exciting journey when I became the executive director of the Chaldean Cultural Center. That's where you'll find the world's first and only Chaldean Museum—the very one you've just visited through this book.

Would you like to know what I love most about my two special jobs? As a writer, I get to create stories that touch people's hearts, and as a museum director, I get to share our amazing history with young people like you. Every time I tell someone about our past—whether through my books or at the museum—I'm not just teaching them history, I'm helping them discover pieces of themselves they never knew existed.